LAWRENCE & SOPHIA

LAWRENCE

SOPHIA

Doreen Cronin & Brian Cronin

ROCKY POND BOOKS

For Esmé, Abby, and Jack with love

ROCKY POND BOOKS
An imprint of Penguin Random House LLC, New York

First published in the United States of America by Rocky Pond Books,
an imprint of Penguin Random House LLC, 2023

Text copyright © 2023 by Doreen Cronin
Illustrations copyright © 2023 by Brian Cronin

Visit us online at PenguinRandomHouse.com.

Library of Congress Cataloging-in-Publication Data is available.

Manufactured in China
ISBN 9780593618301 • 10 9 8 7 6 5 4 3 2 1
TOPL
Design by Jason Henry • Text set in Filson Pro
The art for this book was created with poster paint on paper.

Lawrence stayed close to home.
He did not go *out there*.

Out there was very big.
Out there was very loud.

Out there was very crowded.

Sophia stayed high off the ground,
traveling from tree to tree.
She did not go *down there.*

Down there was dark.
Down there was bumpy.

Down there was dangerous.

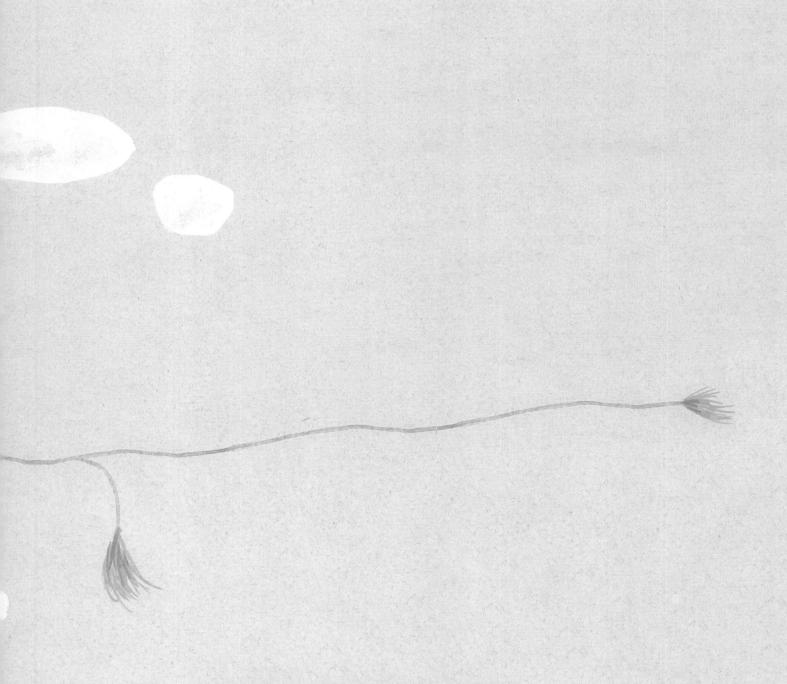

One day, when Sophia was feeling brave,
she took a walk down the longest branch of the tallest tree.
It was the farthest she had ever been from home.

At the other end, she found Lawrence.
No one had ever looked so happy to see her.

No one had ever traveled
so far to see *him*!

When they met outside,
Lawrence stayed in his yard.
Sophia stayed in her tree.

They flew a kite together.

Sometimes Lawrence forgot to stop running.

They played soccer together.
Sophia was always the goalie.

She was not very good.

They put on Sophia's favorite play.
Lawrence always had the same line.

"Rapunzel, Rapunzel, let down your hair."

Sophia moved her nest
to be closer to Lawrence.

Lawrence built a tent
to be closer to Sophia.

They worked side by side
every day.

Almost every day.

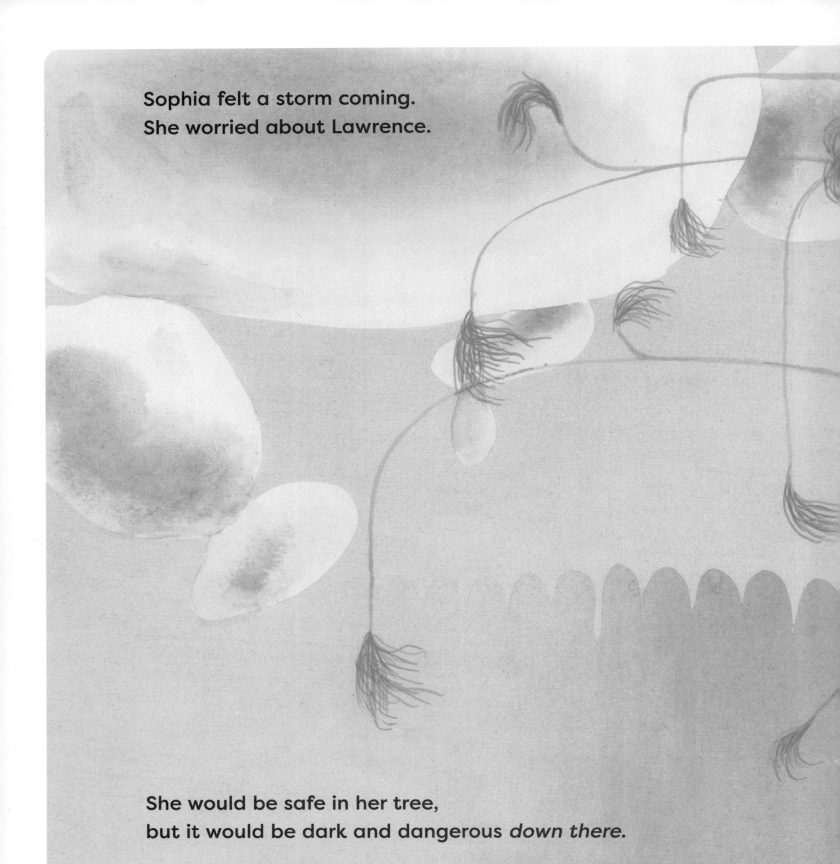

Sophia felt a storm coming.
She worried about Lawrence.

She would be safe in her tree,
but it would be dark and dangerous *down there*.

Lawrence worried about Sophia.

He would be safe and dry in his tent,
but Sophia would be all alone *out there*.

The storm was big.
The storm was loud.

The storm was dark.
The storm was bumpy.

Lawrence?

Sophia was cold.
Lawrence was wet.
The ground was still bumpy.

Lawrence and Sophia didn't notice a thing.

I wonder what's over there?